W9-AUB-982

Breaking
it
Down

RUSTY BARNES

sunnyoutside
Buffalo,
New York

ACKNOWLEDGMENTS

Some of these stories appeared previously in the following journals: *Aesthetica*, Conversely, Dead Mule, Front Street Review, *Literary Potpourri*, Opium, Outsider Ink, Pif, Pindeldyboz, Right Hand Pointing, *Salt Flats Annual*, *SmokeLong Quarterly*, Staccato, Thieves Jargon, and Verbsap.

ISBN-13: 978-1-934513-03-3
ISBN-10: 1-934513-03-2

sunnyoutside
P.O. Box 911
Buffalo, NY 14207
USA

www.sunnyoutside.com

TABLE OF CONTENTS

for
Heather

WHAT NEEDS TO BE DONE

❧

I sat on my mother-in-law's fieldstone porch and snapped green beans into a huge silver bowl. The canning took Ma longer these days. As a dutiful daughter-in-law, I was there to help, no matter what Robbie thought of me anymore. I hinted at our problems sometimes, but Ma just passed it off as something that I should have known before we'd suffered the thrown rice. Robbie drank, Pop had drunk his way into the grave, and Ma suffered it all, canned her veggies, watched her shows, would bury her children with that same stoic look, mouth working in words only she and God could hear.

"Derry," she said, "he'll give it a rest. My boy knows firsthand what drink can do." She leaned off the porch and spat a trail of tobacco juice into the mums. Her unsteady fingers were clasped in her lap, vein-large and brown, caught stiff with arthritis, she said.

"I know." I said it the way I was supposed to say it, with a catch in my voice. "It's just been so long."

I couldn't wait to leave, but I spent my days there doing what had to be done, making sure that Ma and her younger boys, Jimmy and my Purl, were fine. The boys didn't need it. They were sixteen and nineteen, rawboned and clumsy the way farm boys are. They felt as awkward as I did, this town woman married to their brother. They knew I'd been born to do something other than stick patiently by their sweaty brother and his tedium: alcohol and oats, hay and mastitis. I thought so too and everyone unfortunately knew it. Robbie certainly did—he'd stopped paying attention to me about a year after we had first gotten married. When he started buying a fifth a day.

"Boys probably need help in the barn," Ma said. "They should have been able to bale the north field." She said it as if there were still a south field, as if they would make money when the barn still held most of last year's bales. She made to get up from her perch on the toolbox, but slowly. We'd been snapping beans for a couple hours.

"I'll go," I said. "Don't get up, Ma." I thought of Purly in the dry air and barn-must, wanting a drink of cool water. He looked nothing like Robbie. He had ideas though, and Robbie had drowned his last one years ago.

"So you will," she said. "Only woman I ever knew

who baled hay as much as you was my ma. And she had to." I flicked a glance at her, wondering what was behind that tiny knowing smirk on her tobacco-brown lips.

"We all have things we have to do, Ma." I turned back and threw the last few beans into the pot at her feet. "And some of us never get to do them." I glanced back once more as I walked away, and I could see all those beautiful yellow flowers, heavy with Ma's brown spit, dripping onto the ground.

Jimmy was fiddling with the elevator, attaching the belts to the tractor engine. He had a plastic milk jug of water at his feet. I picked it up and he leaned over me. "Funny, Derry. Even when I'm so damn thirsty I could spit dust you never bring me water in the loft."

"Grow up, Jim."

"I could drink a whole gallon of water right now, I bet, and never come up for air." He looked me over once, as if I was a tool that needed fixing. He returned to the belts, and I took the fifteen-foot ladder into the loft as if I did it every day, which I did. He yelled after me, over the engine noise. "It'll be at least a half-hour before this wagon's finished."

Purl had laid the blanket out already, wisps of hay stuck to his hairless chest. As I loosened his jeans, it wagged at me like a finger, an accusation I could never answer to anyone's satisfaction but my own.

"Derry," he said, "I've been waiting." And I felt for him, and thought of Robbie, every time. The wrongness seemed right; every time I swore not to do it again, for all its rightness. Yet it continued to happen and I continued to know that I should stop it. But I had been a dutiful wife, daughter-in-law, sister-in-law, and now I had done something for me. The family, the world, could go to hell. I'd gone from girl to wife with no transition. No days of going buck-wild in the way the boys could. Purly just wanted me, and he didn't care how or when or who was around or how much he'd had to drink or whether he would be able to get to the package store before it closed. I could feel Purly's throbbing pulse beneath my lips, his life, a life that included me.

When we eventually caught up with the bales spewing forth from the elevator, I went down the ladder backward, a sweet ache between my thighs, and saw Robbie had come home, his pickup parked, hood up already, and a mess of beer cans strewn in the dirt drive.

"Boys," Robbie said. He barely looked my way.

"Hi baby," I said, smelling the whiskey as I walked toward him, the odor like a second skin. I leaned up to kiss him and I felt him tremble as I caught his lower lip between my teeth. He pulled away, and I could feel their eyes hot on my back. I knew that even if Ma or Robbie never found out about Purly and me, if I pretended at love like a schoolgirl and never told them a thing, if I continued on with the way things were done, it would never be enough.

Thirty years of snapping beans, of lying placid and pretending joy while drunken Robbie poked away at me occasionally in the dead of night, thirty years of chaff in my hair and beard-rash on my cheeks, a fell row of farm children and the knowledge of my deliberate choices creased forever in my forehead, I reached for Robbie's hand, and I saw Purly tense, and I stopped.

Ma stood cross-armed by the rusted fence, mumbling to herself. She didn't look my way; instead, she looked at Jimmy and Purl, who were behind us, pushing and slapping at each other. "Hi brother," Jimmy said. He stiffened and pushed his hands into his back pockets. Purly looked away at the sidehill. I knew then that neither Ma nor Jimmy, Robbie nor even sweet Purl, would understand that I was doing what needed to be done.

CERTITUDE

Mathilde knew that Warren wanted nothing more than to be feral, a slavering beastly man prone to sudden rages, a man who might chase down a kill with great loping strides like a wolf, neatly hamstring it, and howl his success to the stars. She knew this with certitude and no little anxiety, as women know things about their husbands that they can never touch or affect. Out there, just beyond their comfortable suburban home, their daughter Violet had gone to smoke marijuana with her friends, and Warren had caught her by the sound of her giggle when he had stepped into the woods to urinate after raking the leaves, and after chasing away her friends

Bobby and Tito, had summarily disowned her and thrown her out on her teenaged rump.

Warren had not always been this way, never so quick to passion and short of intellect. Mathilde recalled him as she had known him for most of their twenty years together, a lanky man with a slight gut who could put a new clutch plate in the car at noon and watch an opera that same night. She recalled every detail of their five-year engagement, their eventual decision to have Violet—her name an obvious Verdi homage—and all the various and sundry elements of a life lived together, and generally lived well.

She could point to the spot where Warren had begun to be different, too—that day in June when his eyes changed; that night when he had made love to her with such force as to be brutal, and had rolled off her and began to weep into his pillow; that sudden need to be by himself late at night when she might have preferred to fall asleep on his shoulder while watching a late movie; all of these things she could point to but not quite understand; what was it she had done, after all?—but she could only watch him now, arms tightly woven across her chest—not daring yet to speak—as he put Violet out into the driveway like a rug-wetting puppy, tossing her suitcase behind her and throwing his skinny arms up in what she imagined was a gesture of dismay.

Mathilde sobbed as she watched Violet leave in her raggedy Civic, yet could not think of how to stop her husband without ruining what little self-esteem he had remaining. She knew behind his eyes he thought of himself as another person now, and that Violet's teenaged scheming and furtive rendezvous with those pimply boys in baseball caps and heavy gold chains at the end of their private drive signified something more to him than mere rebellion. Mathilde could see the life Warren wanted to live reflected in Violet's actions, as if he believed that smoking pot would be only the first step in a long and sorry run of recidivism that in his suffering he actually wanted to share. Maybe in Warren's mind Violet would end up in Sturgis on the back of a Harley-Davidson, swilling Jack Daniels, indiscriminately fucking, howling at a gibbous moon. And so it became Mathilde's responsibility to save them both from what they wanted.

After he threw Violet out, Warren disappeared into the cellar, where he had installed a 54-inch flat-screen television as a joking reference to a midlife crisis. He spent nearly all his free time there these days. He owned a large number of operas and obsessively taped episodes of *Big-Game Hunter* and *Killer White-Water* and filed them in date-of-show order in the cherry cabinet beside the television.

Mathilde crept down the stairs in her slippers, expecting him to be lost somewhere in the Grand Tetons or deep into the opening of a Puccini or Verdi. She saw him sitting there in his undershirt, holding their phone in his hand, and she thought of how best she might accomplish a connection in his fragile state, and chose what she knew would appeal most, shedding first her housecoat, then her nightgown, now her slippers. Warren she could save.

Naked, she stood before him as a sob rose in his chest. She took the phone from his hand and lowered herself onto him. Even in his pain she could feel him stir beneath her, and it was no trick at all after so many years of marriage to put him deeply inside her with minimal effort, and less a trick to take his head and firmly press it between her breasts as he convulsed.

As her breath came harder so did his, and she let the phone fall from her fingers to the sofa and grasped his head again with both hands, lifted it and kissed away his tears. He began to laugh and cry at the same time, and Mathilde knew that she had managed to catch whatever spark of him had been about to leave her for something else, something more nebulous, and the phone rang.

Warren sat upright quickly, but she continued to move against him, eyes closed, continued to let the phone ring in spite of the cramp developing in her left thigh, continued for a long slow few seconds until she felt him begin to grind against her. She heard the telltale click as the answering machine picked up and she felt him tighten, then slump bonelessly. Mathilde was grateful that it had become their habit to turn the volume down after a certain hour. She felt Warren's breath against her breast, and a knot of pain moved in her leg, and she kissed the top of his head and didn't let herself wonder who had called, or what the mysterious caller might have said.

THE GREAT
RESPONSIBILITY

⚜

Carlos Bob lives and sleeps in the backmost room of the modular addition of a trailer in the Whispering Pines Trailer Court. He's a confused boy, not only because of his name, some ethnic mismatch his mama dreamed up with her girls before she fell asleep with the plastic tube around her arm still. He's confused because his little sister is missing since this morning, and no one seems to want to find her. Mama's girlfriends left a while ago, smirking among themselves and bumping into each other before peeling out in the dirt drive, and Sissy, the big one, patted him on the head and told him to be a good little hero. He said he would, but he doesn't feel much that way right now, more like his belly's shaking.

He huddles in a pool of blankets on the top bunk with his Spiderman comics and dreams of being able to rip the side of the trailer and walk into the storm of life out there, rain sheeting off his skin-tight red and blue suit like a movie. He will find her somewhere in a nameless city with dark foreboding streets and a garish street lamp where brain-dead lug-muscled thugs will try to stop him, no match for his web-wrapped fists and keen spider-senses. He will whip his way through them like Mama does the cobwebs when she cleans.

Tanya is not so little, he guesses as he jumps down from the bunk bed. She's a big girl for her age, which is four. She doesn't talk much yet, but likes to walk through the neighbor's flower garden, and normally Carlos Bob goes with her, but today he has chosen to stay inside and draw Spidey and Doc Ock and Venom, and Tanya has not come back. He's worried too about Mama, who is lying in the middle of the sofa. It looks as if she's thrown up a little bit, and he lifts the edge of her shirt—pale fishy skin—and wipes off her mouth.

Daddy Bill will come home soon from the university with Tanya, Carlos Bob hopes, and will turn off Mama's weird music that she plays during the day, maybe take them out for thick cheeseburgers and fries not too hot to hold in your hand. By the time they come home Mama will be awake and will have cleaned the ashtrays of their gunk and pulled her hair back, and they will all sit on the couch together and drink pop while they watch cartoons on video. But he should get Tanya first.

Carlos Bob opens the screen door, holds it carefully and doesn't let it slam for fear of waking Mama. He steps out onto the green long-haired lawn, still wet from the rain, and cuts across the board bridge over the drainage ditch, where he and Tanya floated his plastic boats yesterday. He can see the tugboat trapped at the edge of the fall, moving over and over. He steps into the knee-deep water and tosses the tiny boat onto the grass, and while he does he catches a hint of red at the corner of his vision, and steps over to the slight fall knowing already what he will see, the back of Tanya's tiny skirt bobbing madly in the brown water below.

He jumps down in to pick her up and doesn't realize how deep it is, and he's over his head and struggling a little. He thinks of what Spidey would do, imagines being able to capture air inside a balloon of spider-silk, imagines pulling his sister in and letting her breathe it, and he wishes it were true, he can almost touch her, and the water closes over his sight, when he feels a hand on the back of his shirt and feels himself hauled into the air, and he coughs dirty water onto the grass.

When he wipes his eyes clear he can see Daddy Bill bent over Tanya a little ways away. Daddy's cursing to himself, and she's still there silent, her bag lunch still tied to her dress-sash. He can smell the banana in her lunch, and he knows it's next to the PBJ and Little Debbie snack cake, because he packed it for her, with a smiling Spidey on a napkin, so she would know she would be safe. Carlos Bob wishes the thing would all end, wishes Mama would wake up and hold him and Tanya too, but Daddy Bill is just sitting there now watching the water run from Tanya's mouth.

He remembers the music this morning, Mama and Tanya and him, swaying and singing about flowers and hairs and eyes, and the thought of Tanya walking through the water, the marigolds tucked behind her ears like two big orange eyes, like the antenna-eared aliens they saw on TV, would be more than OK. Would be cool. There is still a chance she will get up and walk to him, he thinks, and he will encase her forever in the protective cocoon of web he has prepared for the great responsibility sisters are, and there they'll stay together telling stories until Mama or Daddy Bill come to unwrap them gently and put them to bed.

No One Left
to Care About
the Fat Man

The sky is poison, winter blue. I can see my breath. Jackie is at the end of the road, and the music from the radio—classic rock, of course, where the 70s and 80s never end, like an IHOP for chrissakes—is going to take me wherever she is on one long brutish chord. I want somewhere quiet, where we can sit on someone's porch and drink bitter iced tea and wait for the world to stop. But it won't happen. The vision blurs as I think about finding her. I left my last check on the table in case she comes back; since she's gone I'd have no way to cash it anyway. I can get a job in Peeburgh and save enough to get the rest of the way.

The Peter Pan terminal in Buxton isn't even a terminal, more the side of a building with a plastic awning and a small alcove where there's a single yawning old lady ticket-taker who doubles as the receptionist at the unemployment office around the corner. My father's probably in there signing up for the winter, where I ought to be. As the weather changes, my job and his disappear. Can't work outside in the snow. I can't stand this place. I feel like soon I'll be someone like him, or Velma, who's been there forever. She's got thin red-dyed hair and curly nails, and she says ninety bucks will get me to Pittsburgh, sure enough, which is nearer to Kentucky and Jackie than I am now, so it'll work. She pats my hand and I can see the loose skin shake on her upper arm.

Jackie said she'd leave, but I wasn't smart enough to listen. She said stay home, Buddy. Stay home and be with me. I came home last night dogging it from work, and I stopped to pick up some strawberry wine for her, so we could have a nice dinner, I got behind a wreck, and things just progressed, and I was late. Not fucking up.

"Buddy, you son-of-a-bitch." She's curled up on the couch, her feet underneath her, a pile of butts in the tray already. It's only been two hours. There's a suit-case beside her.

"I got behind a wreck. Two cars. Blood everywhere. What's that?" It's the scene she wants. For me to pay more attention. It's not as if I haven't been here before.

"You work so late, Buddy. I don't know what you want." I can see her hand trembling. I want to punch

29

her, leaving me like this. For nothing. It's supposed to be about something.

"I brought some strawberry wine for your leaving me." I kick my boots off against the door.

"Do you want me?" There's the million-dollar question, so I hand her the bottle of wine. She throws it against the wall where it thumps once and rolls around on the tile, comes to rest near the cat food bowl. "Do you fucking want me?"

"Yes." I haven't even gotten my coat off yet.

"No you don't." Jackie walks into the bedroom and throws the door open behind her, where it bangs against the wall and leaves a hole I'll have to patch again this weekend. "If you want me, come in and fucking take me."

When I go in after her, she's already naked from the waist down. "I don't want to do this, Jackie," I say. Truth is she's turning me on and I don't want to be turned on. I want to hold onto this mad for a while, see where it takes me. I want to know if this is the moment we both need, where we can both say fuck it safely, without conscience, be done with this wreck of a marriage.

"Look at me," she says, voice shaking with hurt. "I shaved the way you wanted me to." Her bush is gone, just a little strip of hair like an eyebrow. I mean, I might have mentioned it'd be hot once. I didn't want this. Her face is a crisis. I am a crisis.

"Jackie. Just don't." Soon as my mouth opens I regret saying it, and as I know it will her face collapses. I go in to take a leak, to let her calm down, and I hear the door slam before I can shake it off. As I stand there, I decide to wait the night out—she's done this before, and so have I—I can feel this one might be different, but I've decided to pretend not to care. The night is dark, and Jackie is a light somewhere in it, fading soon. But still a light.

I know now she's gone to Kentucky, to Louisville, to her people that she's always talking about that I would never understand. Good suburban RV-driving folks. Dad wasn't home when I called for a ride, so it took me two hours to walk to the Buxton bus station. I wonder how far she's gotten since last night. Down by the corner of the awning, a fat man's pants are down, and he's pissing against the wall. Velma must be back at the unemployment office. There's no one left to care about the fat man as the bus rumbles up.

I don't know what I'll find in Louisville, but I have to go. Before that I'll be stranded in Pittsburgh. Piss-burg. There's just Jackie somewhere down the road, this woman I may or may not love, and I'm following the Appalachian Mountains down to find her. I mean, with absolutely *dick* to show, and no one to tell about it anyway.

BEAMER'S OPERA

Every morning when Beamer milked the cows he sang from his favorite operas, attaching the nozzles to their bags and patting them each on the flank, bursting into vibrato-laden songs of despair and longing while his hands were occupied with his very necessary tasks. He imagined the cows with their deep brown eyes and kind souls were listening to him as he roared forth regret and lust and love and sorrow in an alien tongue. Beamer named his bulls Stentor and Cadenza, and cried when Stentor had to be butchered, and realized then that his time on earth grew shorter by the aria.

He was sixty-two years old and fortunate. He had seen Pavarotti and had been to Italy and stood in a grove of olives trees and imagined himself Christ on the Mount giving lessons to the people and had loved himself in that guise. He imagined he could have done well, but cows and sheep and Guinea hens and Rhode Island Reds were not able to be converted, and he had no little children to suffer unto anyone, and Alicia and he were long past childbearing years, yet he felt the pull when the cows gave birth and he extended his arm into them to help the calf forth in the way he had never helped a child of his own, and it hurt, and so he sang as he pulled forth the sloppy calf and slimy bag, with all his heart.

Beamer lived with Alicia, though he was not married to her, because she was a woman who did not enjoy opera, and so he sang to himself at odd moments throughout the day as he repaired fence and trundled his barrow full of tools from place to place on the small farm he owned, but never to Alicia in the house. She tolerated Beamer's interest, but did not understand his tears when Stentor died, nor pretend to like the screeching and whining she heard in Mozart and Verdi and even in the Gershwin *Porgy and Bess* that he sometimes stooped to in his weak moments.

He lived this way for years and lived well, and Alicia passed before him with a quiet sigh in the middle of the night and Cadenza, too, covered his last cow and became burger, and still he sang though the grass grew long and he could no longer do his work himself and hired it done with a man named Sam who chewed tobacco and spat into the drop all day long, but who was honest and forthright and knew that Beamer wanted to sit quietly in the midst of the animal heat in the pasture and hum his songs of regret and lust and love and sorrow, and not be bothered by the details of his ending life.

Beamer loved the cows, and the chickens pecked round his feet and he could see all the days of his life laid out before him as some carpet and he could count them and measure the worth in every single thread, and so he did. He raised his arms and stood from his lawn chair and began to sing again in a low quavering voice, thinking of Stentor and Cadenza and even of Alicia, and the cows milled around him as if he had called to them from the Mount to listen, and hesitatingly the cows stood upon their hind legs and danced a slow and ponderous dance, due to their extreme weight and breadth, and Sam watched from inside the milkhouse and knew all the emotions of Beamer. He stood incredulous as the cows made a slow and somehow graceful procession around the old and singing man, and Sam spat into the drop and still they danced, and when Beamer ceased to sing and sat heavily in his chair the cows nosed at their grass as if nothing had happened, and Beamer's head dipped into his chest. Sam watched him. A single cow came up and snuffled in Beamer's

shirt as if looking for food, and then walked slowly
away, switching her tail.

THE CONSCIENCE SPEAKS

When you speak to your ultrasound the way new fathers do, Pink the Harley-Davidson Motorcycle Man, be sure to speak loudly, because the doctors in the room cannot hear you. They are busy with Steffie, the woman you have impregnated. Who knew when you wrapped her up in your big blanket that night and did it on the park bench under cover while the cute coeds and their boyfriends stood nearby and gawped at the children passing by, that you would soon have one of your own? Who could have ever guessed in this late 20th century that Steffie would be an old-fashioned kind of girl, who would let you do it all right, but would not fess up to the nasty truth, which was that she was not on the pill? You maybe would have done it anyway, you devil-may-care, ride-to-live, live-to-ride, bugs-in-your-teeth guy, but you have to wonder, because I'm making you wonder, because that's what I do.

And now you are off your bike and in this sterile room with Steffie and Doctor Faust, a smiling black woman with huge hands, waiting to see what God hath wrought.

Doctor Faust says *look there* and you do, and Steffie cranes her neck sideways to look at the monitor, and you see a blob and what may or may not be an arm, but looks like a Rorschach blot, and you want to say *it's a tall ship, mast broken and falling*, or maybe *a rain cloud shot through by a thunderbolt*, and instead you say, *yes Stef, look there, the little guy's giving us a power-fist.*

Steffie glares at you then, cradling her belly, avoiding the gel smeared just above her pubic hair, and then I have to tell you what she means, because she doesn't want to emasculate you in front of the doctor, that the fetus could as easily be a girl, and you feel guilty then, because you want a boy, if you have to have one at all, and you just don't get how everything has shifted now, do you?

So Doctor Faust moves the wand a bit, and the blacks turn to grays and whites and you lose the thing that might be an arm and next you see a howling skull in front of you on the monitor, and the attending nurse clicks a switch and Doctor Faust says, *there, we got its little face*, and Steffie speaks for the first time, says, *O God, Pink, its face*, and all you can think of is that machine pumping radiation in tiny doses through the tiny fetus which combined with the presumably normal birth, a normal life, will give your tiny future child a bulbous head and tiny sticklike arms, and you're already in the cancer ward of Children's Hospital ten years later pulling your no-longer-long hair out and cursing God, watching your child waste away, and I have done this to you, because it's what I must do, because otherwise I'm not going to get anything through your damned thick skull, now am I, Pink? Things have changed.

Steffie is up now and nearly dressed and giving you dirty looks because she knows like I know that you've been off in the stratosphere and paying shitty attention. Pink, you have the little computer photo in your hand and you are not moving, and I understand that, because I'm finally getting through to you, the least little bit of knowledge has cracked your brainpan and buddy, you've had eight-and-a-half months—it's about time. So you load her onto your Harley now and cinch her helmet tight, and put your leather jacket around her even though it doesn't fit, and you head back down to the park bench on the beach, my friend, because your behavior in all this has been shit-ty, and you need to make it up to her with a big sundae. You did remember the sickness, right? How this is the only thing she can keep down? Nice. You may get through this alive.

Now listen to me, Pink. This is the last ride you take on the Hog, much as you both love it, much as the wind in your face feels right, much as you'd love to have her on the park bench again—pregnant as she is she's still a little exhibitionist; you're amazed you still wants to do it—you won't, because her big belly is against your back, and as you hit fourth gear you can feel her rock back with the weight of the bike and settle forward, and you can feel the tiniest of kicks in your middle back—dude, you are so stupid some-times—you realize that it's not Steffie's heart the way you feel it sometimes tripping against you, it's somebody else now, booting at you for attention and so you slow it down, just a bit, and you look around with new eyes at the darkened street, the sun setting past the beach, brown with rain, and you go down into third gear. Maybe you're getting it, finally, Pink the Harley-Davidson Motorcycle Man. Maybe you're finally getting it.

THUNDER
& PUTSY

٭

Rip Sanderson woke up headsore, jeans heavy with blood. Along about 1:30 a.m., as nearly as he could tell, his redbones, Thunder and Putsy, had treed a coon after a forty minute run on the logging road on the steep sidehill by Prutsman's. He knew that had to be where he was, though the low dark of early morning was so long off he wouldn't be able to tell anything for a while. He remembered them jumping at the tree, slavering and baying, he remembered its eyes glowing, and he remembered the branch falling into his face, the coon with it. The .22

on his hip had gone off and the bullet burned straight through his thigh like fire, his leg had given like a dry stick and he'd crab-slid his way down the hill, grabbing for anything to stop the stumble. Then his head struck something. He'd been out for a while, and he couldn't find an exit hole for the bullet. Putsy lay at his feet, one eye missing, her face and throat a mass of torn flesh and hair. Rip could see the slight rise and fall of her chest, punctuated by an occasional rattly whine. He couldn't see Thunder anywhere, and he couldn't stand. Putsy whined again, her tail thumping weakly against the ground. He hunkered next to her, trying to buy some of her warmth in the early November cold. He scratched her head where his fingers could find whole flesh and considered his situation.

Randi would wake soon and wonder where he was, and now he'd lost a dog and probably time from work for this, because he hadn't called anyone up to go with him. Rip took his coon-hunting seriously, even to the point of doing the almost-communal act himself instead of with Jim and Billy. In the dead of night, dogs baying, running in pursuit of one of the meanest and most human-like animals he'd known, he found a sort of purpose that he felt might be akin to going to war. You had one purpose in the hunt, and everything else fell by the wayside like so many fingernail parings. Putsy's low whine was constant now, and he wished he could do something for her.

He'd stopped hunting with blueticks and moved to the redbones years ago now. Blueticks could be distracted; hunting was a game to them. Rip had spent hours running them down the road, their leaders shut in his driver-side door, the slow crawl of his car more than they could take sometimes, where he'd have to stop before he dragged them to death at five miles an hour. He'd given them an old coon to chew up once. He'd let it out of the cage and waited for the three silly pups to tear it up, but they sat grinning happily at him, tongues lolling even while the coon hissed. Thunder, on the other hand, had broken his chain loose from its nail on the tree and torn across the yard with blood on his mind. Only then had the blueticks taken the hint and joined in the bloodletting.

Putsy's breathing grew more labored as Rip sat next to her. He pulled at his blood-sodden pants pocket to get at the gun, and realized his fingers were too cold and his leg too stiff and painful to get at it. Putsy's voice had been like a church bell, heard from a township away. She and Thunder were the best dogs he'd ever had. Rip realized they were past tense already; already he was building the memory trove for the next dog, the next story, the next clean shot he'd have at a hissing man-pawed beast, with some other dog at the bole of the tree. It felt like betrayal and he hadn't even done the deed yet, the pistol lying against his thigh like an accusation.

Morning would come, but Rip knew Putsy wouldn't make it. He knew he should dig the .22 out of his pocket and put the dog down, but he couldn't get at the gun, he told himself, without the blood flowing even more. And he was in pain; he'd lost blood. He thought once he heard Thunder's deep-voiced bay, and even Putsy had pricked up an ear, but he didn't turn up. It would have been a comfort. He laid his head on her heaving flank and closed his eyes and fever-dreamed those sad old blueticks, undoubtedly someone's pet now, each of them. Good dogs, for some things, but Thunder and Putsy twice their worth. Putsy's chest spasmed underneath his ear.

When he woke up, Putsy's body was cold and the fog across his brain had lessened somewhat. He heard a noise in the brush and turned to see Randi, leading Thunder. She'd brought Jim with her. It was easy for them to figure out what had happened, and Thunder had licked Putsy about the face once or twice, then

Rip. As they had shoulder-supported him down the steep ridge to where they'd left his truck, he could feel that pistol against his hip still, even though the thing was now unloaded and in Jim's pocket. His dog was back on the ridge, and the bullet that should have been hers rattled now in Jim's jacket, and Rip's mind filled with his own pain. He imagined the sharp short crack and the snap of her head against the ground, and felt nothing but shame.

CLASS

W hen your neighbor James Frehley cusses
you out for hanging a block and tackle
from the silver maple in your front lawn,
begin to pull the engine from your Galaxie anyway,
smile and nod to him in his chaise longue. Offer him
a Bud. Reach the hand of human kindness across the
wide expanse of manicured shrub separating the two
of you, and as he sputters his refusal, nod at him again
and continue what you were doing, pretending he is
not there across his finely-turfed lawn and sprinkler
system with his two lovely children, twins even, and
his tanned and large-breasted wife who mows the
lawn in her bikini and sweats profusely as you watch

her through the kitchen window.

When Mrs. Frehley—God, don't call me that, she says, smiling through her tears—sniffs at you as she picks up her mail, you in your sweaty cutoffs and green ankles, using your weedwhacker to clear out the broadleaf dock growing around your mailbox, smile kindly at her and remember: God rewards the meek. As she and her step-daughter Belinda come by and knock on the screen door while you're watching Carmen Del Toro and Bunny Bleu in *Hometown Kink*, pull the couch pillow over your prominently swollen member and yell to her that you do not want any fucking cookies, thank you very much, and please get the fuck out of my house, even though they are technically not in it.

Listen carefully as Timmy and Belinda, those noxious twin terrors of eight-year-olds, sneak through the hole in the shrubbery and throw pine cones at your mastiff/pit bull mix, Spud. Pay careful attention as Spud lunges to the end of the logging chain you've bolted to the side of your garage and connected as well to a railroad tie driven three feet into the soft loam of your backyard. Imagine Spud slavering at them, running to the end of the brown dirt circle of lawn his incessant pacing has claimed for his own, rimmed with grand piles of week-old shit and the remnants of chewed plastic bowls and battered iron ones.

When you've finally finished the Galaxie, start it up and listen to the engine, watch it belch black smoke into the air, and determine that your timing is off. Say fuck it and go back inside to watch the videotape of your wedding over and over again. Wonder where that fellow went. You know where the wife went, after all. Cry tears of joy that you are shut of the neighbor-fucking bitch, and tears of abject sorrow and self-pity that she left with everything that mattered, and tears of mirth that even your best friend-neighbor-buddy Jimmy Frehley, for all his goatee and manners and six-pack abs, will not be able to keep her either. Fall asleep on the sofa with snot on your pillow and in your mustache.

As the morning finds you vomiting into the sofa cushion, determine a plan of action, any action. Wait until James Frehley leaves for work. Walk over to his lovely home and stride into his foyer with Spud on your weakest leash. Tie Spud to the banister with a slipknot. Feed him raw meat and stool softener. Cover his nose in turpentine. Get him really pissed off, and as Amy Frehley, your former wife, comes out of the bathroom naked, shaking out her blonde hair, don't even notice her obvious beauty. Simply throw her an old t-shirt and a pair of period panties, the only thing she left behind besides you. Make her mow your lawn with your pushmower. You won't need to hold your twelve-gauge on her; she'll do it because she knows how you people are; she's seen *Deliverance*, *Natural-Born Killers*, *Kalifornia*. Never mind that you haven't owned a gun in years. She just knows. And cries and does what she is told.

Imagine for once that these people know you, that the meek do inherit the earth. Imagine that God cares.

GROSS IMPERFECTIONS

Tory Sullivan lived in a crack between now and then, a long-armed brown-eyed hippie woman, tall enough to be seen over the wheel but too short for most anything else. She drove a Taurus so rusted you could see through the driver-side door where her skirt was hiked. You could set your fantasy to her twice-weekly trips. Every grocery boy and cart-hauler would find a reason to be at the front of the store when she checked out. You never saw so many eager baggers in your life, and I tried to be one of them, but subtle-like, because the manager only helped when things got quick, when the cashiers were gum-snapping young and the lines moved like the bakery department in midweek, which is to say not at all. My name is Richard Norcutt, and I was the front-end supe on this day. I heard it first from Gabby, who chain-smokes Newports by the bottle return machine, who whistled at me and then turned away as if she really didn't care that I cared. Then I heard the death-rattle of the Taurus as it pulled into the handicapped space at the front of the store, and the door slammed and the woman herself appeared, head bobbing in the window like a pigeon.

Tory Sullivan, my God. If you could have seen the way her left calf sank into her sandal through the hole in her car door you would have been in love too, like us. She tromped in the front door, leaning heavy-right on her short leg. No one knew why one leg was shorter than the other—who could ask about such a thing?—and the thing was, no one cared. We loved her for that gross imperfection, for the purposeful swing of her hand as it pushed in the door and for the faint sheen of perspiration under her arms, for the ungraceful stutter of her step and the crow's wing beside her eye, for the incontrovertible proof that God did not exist. We were pimpled and jangly with caffeine and desperately in love with Tory, who was in pursuit of eggs and tampons and puppy chow, not the admiration of future busboys and middle-managers and computer technicians. I would have been her terrier, yapping at her heel for weeks on end for a biscuit opportunity, I would have been her dog, with apologies to Iggy, and I had a plan.

Chris from hardware nabbed her puppy chow, Johnny the head cashier her eggs, even Crystal our token dyke got there before me and handed her a bonus pack of breath mints as a last-minute gesture, but I held the ace in my spot, at the loss-prevention station next to the scratch tickets, watching everyone who came and left. I would be the last person she saw as she exited the Shaw's, and I would say something to her worth recalling, and she would bring her eyes up from under that broad-brimmed hat and she would say something back, and something would happen between us, and before I could speak she paid, looked past me, exhaling deeply, and passed by, breaking my heart. I would have the rest of forever to consider how it would be to search in the crack between my nows and thens for her, for Tory who I admired from afar, who breathed in my direction that day, and left by saying "God you are so *creepy*."

PRETTY

Kathleen wants to make a stand, wants to let Brady know that what he's done is fucked up, plain and simple. Safeword, hell. What kind of safeword is *pretty*? She's had ample time to think about it as she lies on the bed naked and spread-eagled, still wet, still perspiring, waiting for Brady to get off the toilet. Brady is sitting on the toilet with nothing but sweat-socks on, kid-socks really, the white kind with blue stripes at the top, and he looks faintly ridiculous, yet less than five minutes before she'd been bucking like a mule on her knees under him, almost crying with the effort it took not to say the safe-word.

Brady'd tried to force her into it every way he could, hair-pulling, ass-smacking, stopping outright when she was on the brink, but she'd held back from speaking. She wasn't supposed to speak, wasn't supposed to do anything but what he told her to, and they'd agreed on it, but the game took on new meaning when she saw the look in his eyes. He'd warned her, given her a book called BDSM, but she'd barely glanced at it, long enough to see the rigmarole about safewords and mutual trust and submission, long enough to write it off as kink, which she thought she knew about.

Brady sits there, reading a book, just sitting there, whatever business he's done is done, and she decides this will be the first and last time. Topping from below, she'd read it was called, in that kinky novel he'd brought her, the one she'd had to ask him about later on after their second or third vanilla session. She didn't need to ask again after today.

Kathleen gets up and walks into the bathroom, tears the book from his hand and throws it into the tub. Brady says nothing, but winks at her, shrugs his shoulders in a *who-me?* gesture that infuriates her even more, so she reaches down into the front of the toilet, grabs him by the balls with her sharp nails. His eyes widen, though he won't cry out like she did. He is almost instantly erect like a cliché, and she wonders if he feels served now. She digs her nails in, feels sudden warmth on the tips of her fingers. Tonight he'll hurt deep in his crotch like she does. She leans into him, squeezes, whispers, "Say it, goddamn you. Say *pretty*."

FEET OF A DANCER

When Mr. Kleen comes home at night, he takes out his silver hoop earrings and lays them on the desktop by his expensive computer, home page beaming a cross-hatch of light onto his ballet magazines. He runs a hand over his head and feels stubble breeding there. It is like chemo every day, that scrape of blade across his smooth skull, like his wife Charlie dying again, her mouth a gray swale of cancerous rot. He regrets his long-ago decision to shave it for some silly television gig.

He is old now, his trousers must be rolled over his bony ankles, yet the scene must play over and over again: he wakes from sound sleep, perspiring, and hopes again this day to be someone else, to not be the man who must salute a row of a thousand commodes or mug for morons at a store opening in Chillicothe before he takes his midday meal of gin.

Money has not been an issue for some time for Harry Kleen. His place in popular culture is secure, he knows, the products he hawks still first in line at toilet cleaner sales conventions. He has lifted his brawny hands to the Lord and has been blessed. But now he wants more.

Old Harry Kleen still calls himself Harry Blenkowski when he is twenty. His limbs are long and muscular, his concave chest bone a tiny bird, wings outstretched and fluttering under his flesh, most prominent in the very center where his girlfriend Charlie kisses him before he leaves to teach his ballet class. He loves his life and his full head of brownish hair.

As he approaches the barre, he sees a man in a suit with a checkbook and stops cold. "Young man. I have never seen such grace, such ballon. I need you." Harry thinks to himself, yes you do.

In an hour, those honeyed words have his signature on a contract, and Harry tells himself afterward as he holds a grand plié that it will be a boon, that he will be self-sufficient, an artiste, that Charlie will have a dress, no, two, of the finest cuts of silk and already he can see Charlie in a large and floppy hat waiting for him in their new car, her smile a porcelain fount of joy.

It is almost noon now of another working day, and the phone rings once and then cuts off half-through the second ring. Is this the end, Harry asks himself?

Will they miss him when he is gone? He feels of his head, the stubble grown large, he thinks, though his mind knows it is not true. Somewhere Charlie is. But he does not know her anymore, nor his own face as it stares besottedly from his face in the mirror, gin-roses plain to see.

He rises and on gimpy old-man knees turns to face his mirror and lifts his arms allonge. He feels the first pull of his groin as he slides left, his feet still sure underneath him, and he sees himself in a grand jeté. The music in his mind is strong, and it lifts him up and brings him down—his bald head and frail knees, the wide smile that pays his bills—swaying gently in front of his mirror, knowing in his mind that he is graceful and true, that his feet are the feet of a dancer and have always been.

THE
CRASH

Torn up after the car crash, she put her hand on her abdomen, as if she had indigestion. "Yep," she said. "You're going to give birth soon." The tick of the hospital equipment filled the room. She'd been thrown through the window and landed on a guardrail and scraped along for ten feet before coming to rest tummy-first against a concrete piling.

"Not me," I said, but my hand went to my navel anyway. "You're the one's p.g.," I said. I wanted to get back to Ray and the kids, but Shandon was my best friend, and I didn't know how to tell her. She needed me now. She had a lacerated spleen and a slash like a knife-cut along her side where the skin unraveled to a foot-long spot of road-rash. Wear your seatbelt, kids.

"Not any more I'm not," she said. "But it's OK." She coughed once and a little spritz of blood appeared on her hospital johnny, and I thought of all the ways God had to end things, he chose death. He could give us life forever in some other form, some Buddhist thing, where we could go on at least. But he had to make it final.

The doctors said she wasn't continent, and might never be again. She'd want to be dead. I would want to be dead. But she might live. She had to hold onto that. It's what they said.

"Believe me, Carissa," Shandon said. "You're going to have a kid and name it for me and raise it the way a kid ought to be raised. No TV. No snacks but Cheerios and fruit and veggies. Make that baby eat right."

Just then Ray buzzed my cell and I stepped out to take the call, and when I came back Shandon was gone, just blipped out between breaths.

We named our next baby Marta after Ray's mom though. He hated the name Shandon. When he left me nineteen months after Shandon's funeral, I started the process to change Marta's name to Shandon, but it was already too late, and the papers still sit here somewhere, I'm sure.

I take Marta to the graveside and she plays in the flowers. It's where Ray meets us for the court-appointed visitation, because the park's next door. Marta plays in the plastic flowers and Ray stares bullet holes. Shandon lies propped under a stone, gone where I can't see.

I think maybe I'll change my name away from Ray's. Even one minute longer of having that man's name I can't take.

LUCKY
PETE

❧

Woodrow and Little Bill tied balloons to the branches of the silver maple out back of his mother's house and the three of them had fifty bucks riding on who could pop the most. One cylinder each, and Lucky Pete only had to get one, as Bill and Woodrow had squeezed off their shots in rapid succession, and laughing at themselves, gone back to the porch where Marissa was rolling it.

Pete jerked the trigger, but thinking of Marissa—curled up next to the cooler rolling weed—missed his first two because he was a little, just a little, potted already. But Lucky Pete had three more shots, and he determined to get one of the goddamned things, because Marissa watched, and that meant a lot to him right now.

Somewhere over the weeks and months between the open back door that served as the break room at the Sodexho Marriott—where Pete was on grill for the breakfast and lunch rush, eggs over hard and crispy bacon, turkey clubs and pastrami on rye—and the Tipsy Toddler on 4th Street for early afternoon beers that stretched on into twilight, the three of them became friends who competed at everything for Marissa's attention like adolescents. Except the three men were in their thirties and Marissa was a girl who might have been beautiful at sixteen, but had gone to early fat at twenty-two in the way those early maturers often do.

She had an associate's degree in Culinary Arts, long

curly hair and sweet blue eyes, and a rack beyond belief that she kept hidden behind baggy sweatshirts, and it was what was behind those sweatshirts that made Pete unable to concentrate, as those balloons were shaped just so, and when the wind blew strongly, the pink fleshy things hung together in the breeze and quivered like stripper cleavage, and so he missed again, and cursed. He needed to win her over, and couldn't talk the way Woodrow and Little Bill did, all smooth and easy. He had to win her like a knight won some fair lady in King Arthur's time. He squeezed the trigger one more time and saw a branch disappear, but the balloons still waved, and he couldn't imagine how it might be to actually catch her attention. What would he do with a twenty-two-year old woman anyway?

Woodrow and Little Bill didn't mince words. On their breaks they knelt by the back door with cigarettes cupped in their hands and coughed loudly when Marissa came out back for ice.

Oh Missy. You fine thing. Marissa baby. What up, my baby dog, little poodle puppy baby.

Marissa grinned her lopsided grin at them, shook their hands when they offered them, maybe gave them a brief hug sometimes, but continued on her way, and Pete let the eggs go hard and the bacon sizzle as he watched her stand on a chair to dump the ice, following the strip of flesh at her waist revealed when she leaned over the soda machine to fill it. He didn't feel like he was in love, but certainly interested to a fault, and Woodrow and Little Bill noticed.

"Pete. She too fine for you. Lucky white SOB."

Pete wiped his hands on the front of his apron and watched her as she went back to the cash register, where the old men handed her fistfuls of change for their toast and coffee and where Pete remembered he would soon have to break out the rye and pumpernickel loaves.

Pete could hear laughter behind him now, and the dope-smell reached him and made him more nervous. He hoped his Mom wouldn't be home soon. He raised his arm and sighted slowly on the balloons, began to squeeze the trigger when Marissa appeared right by his shoulder. She moved so close to him he could smell her shampoo and she breathed slightly on his neck and he tensed.

"Don't miss," she said, and slapped him on the ass, and the shot went off, and a piece of pink balloon appeared at the end of the branch.

Little Bill came over then whooping and hollering, and grabbed Pete by the arm and swung him around. Marissa stood by with her arms crossed, a shit-eating grin on her face, and Woodrow offered him the joint and Pete took it, and he saw the balloon pop again in his mind, all an accident. Marissa's fault, but he couldn't find it in his heart to blame her, and he was fifty bucks richer after all.

He sat on the porch and drank and smoked and watched Woodrow and Little Bill and Marissa play Strip Monopoly. Nobody seemed to be losing clothes, so he got up and staggered into the bathroom.

Lucky Pete, he said to himself as he looked in the mirror. At a party where nobody got naked playing Strip Monopoly, even Marissa with the big breasts. Where the grass was good, but people couldn't shoot straight.

Pete knew this: he didn't want to be where the bad luck was anymore. He sighed, ran a hand through his hair and went back outside to the party, where the noise already sounded miles away, where his mother would be home soon to break it all up.

WITNESS

rom Night, 1987. Thesia G. Throckmorton cold-cocked Peter Gee with a fifth of something or other after he'd slid his hand unwanted into the built-in brassiere of her dress. No one believed it, even as the story spread like bad news, her black hair teased up over one eye, blue-toed shoe pointing at his unit as if to say one more word motherfucker, one more word, but it happened. I was it, the only witness to see and spread the news, Peter Gee being unable to move, and Mandy, the girl I was with—God that's another story—passed out in the bed of the truck leaving me sorely bereft, if you know what I mean. Nothing I have seen before or since matched the sight of

Thesia, breasts hanging stutter-puppies, like nothing matched falling in love with her on the spot, a B-movie staple if ever there was one, and me the drive-in movie whore. *Angel Heart* backed with *Hellraiser* had finished playing twenty minutes before, and the only one left in the cavernous field besides us was Toddy Martin, unconnecting and rolling speaker wire, locking down the popcorn stand, cursing his hard luck in this shift-draw. Lisa Bonet's bare breasts were much on my mind, and then this, the bloody chicken in my night of high school voodoo. I confess to being less a man than I would have liked in hindsight, helping Thesia out of her high heels and into Mandy's flats, so we could more easily throw Peter up in the back of the truck with Mandy, put their heads resting forehead down on a rolled-up tarp so they wouldn't drown in puke. Yes Lord I took Thesia by the hand and ran, and it was not a dream. I woke in the woods at six a.m., stomach heaving, her head on my thigh, and I knew I had found God and lost God all in one night.

WHAT
FOLLOWS

S tew likes the scent of fresh cat litter, the sun
rising smartly over a ragged tent on the out-
skirts of Karbala—he watches a great deal of
CNN—and a lick or two from his nephew's cherry
vanilla cone on Sundays when he visits his brother in
Hopkinton. A complex man he is not. Stew lives his
life in patterns, one for each block of time and obliga-
tion he must exist in the world for: getting up each
morning for buttered toast and Pepsi; walking no more
than twice around the block until his bowels loosen;
showering first in cold water then in hot; dressing in

the black shirts and black faded pants he has worn in small variation for the last six years. The routines are what sustains him, and have ever since his nerves failed him and he walked out of his former life into this one, a life no less lived-in than the one he had, but infinitely more fraught with catastrophe since that incident six years ago.

Stew freaked out at her. He threw things. He broke windows. He walked out on his job, yes, dumped Editha unceremoniously for Katrinka—half again as old as he was, whom he had fucked for a few hours in a hotel room in New York and conflated the immediate and total gratification of his body with love—certainly, but never as that process unfolded did he imagine that his former life would disintegrate into these small pieces, these deliberately calibrated gestures of normalcy that passed for his life now. Even though Trinka left him, but years after he left his wife—"you are so fucking precise about everything," she had said, flitting off in her snazzy coupe with half his savings and his last bottle of Glenfiddich—and even though he had managed to get another job, nothing was as good as it had been when he was married to Editha.

Editha is in town for a meeting and has agreed to meet with him to finally dispose of their mutual property. Stew thinks he will break out of the cycle today. It's just that it feels so right, with the sun shining high over the refinery towers, his immediate needs dealt with, his clothing hanging off his body just so, seeing the woman who is still technically his wife. This might do the trick, he thinks. Something might be salvageable from his wrecked life.

Editha says she'll meet him in the lobby of the Parker House. It's neutral ground, she says, a high-class outfit where neither of them would ever go in the course of their lives. And I know you'll be on your best behavior there, Stew. He isn't even sure they'll let him through the door without a tie, so he changes into a white shirt with pinstripes left over from his old life, knots a tie carefully around his neck then pulls it loose. He keeps his black pants on.

Stew gets off the subway at Government Center and walks to the Parker House. Along the way he sees at least five women who could be Editha, with their short bobbed hair and long legs. Every time he sees their stockinged legs striding purposely past him, their form-fitting leather jackets and cardigan sweaters loosely knotted, he thinks of how he saw her last, in her sweatpants and a Brett Favre football jersey, packing the backseat of her 4Runner with the last of her clothes and of all things, the broom, dustpan, and mop. The only things she kept from their years together. He's sure there's meaning in that vision if he could stop trembling long enough to consider it.

The Parker House lobby and bar is all black and gold

and gilt edges, crystal wine goblets and the murmurs of the well-off and powerful. He sees her at the bar immediately. Though her hair seems longer, she is not much changed. There is a man with her, and immediately Stew thinks the worst, blood coming to his head and tension to his fists. Then he sees the man is carrying a briefcase. Of course. Why didn't he think to bring his own counsel?

"Hello Stew." She walks over to him purposefully, and surprises him with a brief kiss on his cheek. When she finishes he offers his hand to the lawyer, who says he is Brent, her fiancé.

"Fiancé." Stew smiles uncertainly at Editha, who smiles back. She's had her teeth bleached. Stew notices. "Well, Editha. Congratulations."

Brent speaks for her, says they are both grateful he's decided to meet them. "It won't take long," Brent says.

Stew and Editha agreed on the phone in casual conver-sation, Stew thinks, not as a matter of legality. "Yes. It's fine. It won't take long at all." Stew sits down at the bar, where they are apparently going to take care of the business at hand. Brent and Editha talk. He even hears them and nods appropriately at critical junctures when he is supposed to. In his mind, though, he is in New York City with Trinka, six years ago, fucking away his marriage and his life. He wonders if Trinka ever thinks of him, or if she simply went on with her life the way Editha did.

He signs a paper, several papers, and Brent is up first off the stool tossing down his heretofore-untouched drink. Editha's hand is on Stew's back and she whis-pers in his ear, "I'm glad you're fine, Stew. Have a good life with Katrinka," and for a moment it is all as he has imagined in his mind, minus Brent and the com-ment about Trinka. The corners and edges of his life will be smooth now. Then Editha is shaking his hand

and she and Brent leave.

Stew follows them outside, where they disappear into a cab. He stretches a moment, trying to will the despair from his mind, and feels his throat, where the loose tie has somehow tightened. He takes it off and throws it into a trashcan near the subway. As he pays for his token and descends the rattly old escalator, his eyes film over, and he is alone in a sea of humanity, but moving slowly downward to whatever it is can possibly follow from this.

MISTER
FIXIT

✿

Mister Fixit comes to my house in the middle of the day, though I haven't called him. Rex put his fist through the drywall again last night, and I'm not surprised he's called Mister Fixit. Rex hates to leave things unfinished, unless they're me. He left me cold last night, hot makeup sex gone bad one more time. He didn't kiss me before he left.

"I hear you have stuff need fixing." He tugs at his ball cap in obeisance. Six feet, lanky, brown hair. Like it's been planned this way.

"Did Rex call you?"

"Yes ma'am. Told me you had a hole needed filling."
Mister Fixit has a toolbox in his hand and he's leaning
against the door with the other.

"I have that, yes." This all sounds like a put-on, like
some dumb porn movie. Mister Fixit can't be dumb
enough to not realize what he's said.

"Let me get to filling it, then." It just gets better. He
pushes past me into the kitchen. I wonder for a moment how he knows where to go, but then Rex must
have told him.

I remember then I'm still in my bathrobe. I'm partici-
pating in the cliché now. It seems harmless, to see how
far it will go, how well Rex has prepped Mister Fixit
for what he's about to do. I imagine what Rex might
have said, if this is a game he's picked the players well.

I go upstairs to brush my hair and get some clothes on. I choose tight jeans, a loose t-shirt with no bra. I want to be a cliché now. What's the harm, just once.

I walk back downstairs and into the kitchen, where Mister Fixit is prepping the hole in the drywall, cutting around it.

"Looks like your veneer is peeling too, on that table. You'll need to re-cover that or get a new table."

"That's up to Rex." I brush against him. "Do you want something cool to drink?" He glances at me once with something like amusement in his eyes.

"No thanks, ma'am." He turns back to his hole.

"Sometimes I just want to disappear," I say. "Rex beats me." The tears come.

"Oh ma'am. You don't want to do that. Got a man who loves you." The tears come harder. I can see the hesitation in his eyes. "He'll straighten up," says Mr. Fixit, sympathy in his eyes. He puts the tool down and opens his arms, and I go to him as the script dictates. As he holds me in his smell of body odor and gas, putty and rank man, I can feel myself begin to disappear—it's good. He squeezes tighter, a comfort hug, tighter and tighter. I am smaller and smaller in his arms. I am a wet spot on the shoulder of his grubby shirt, and then I am gone.

DANCE

✲

It was one of those moments of couple therapy where Harley just knew the therapist was in cahoots with Morena, fixing to make his life hell. As if he didn't know what he had done and how it had been wrong, Harley made peace with Morena by agreeing to go and hear what a horrible person he had become, to hang out this thing he called a life on the community clothesline. No one ever parked in the spot in front of New Wings Psychotherapy. Even though the package store and Pudgie's Pizza were there and parking slim in the strip mall, no one wanted the rumors spreading.

"Harley doesn't talk to me." Morena flitting her face with a *Reader's Digest*, rocking back and forth in the chair. "He comes home and turns on the TV."

"Harley." Mercedes said. "You hear what she's saying to you. Go ahead and talk to him, Morena. Not me." Her hospital ID still hung from around her neck. Their appointments were always at the end of the working day, ostensibly so Harley could attend, though most of the time he sat a silent partner, not knowing what he might say to repair a marriage ten years in the ruining, something that he hadn't already said a thousand times, anyway. Women, all their interesting foibles and large breasts, fascinated him.

So Morena turned to Harley and said, "You come home and turn on the TV. I wish you wouldn't."

"Yep." Harley looked at his nails, then out the window, and let out a breath he hadn't realized he'd been holding. "You're right." He wondered how other men handled themselves. Theoretically everyone didn't sleep with every woman they were interested in. But even lust of the heart was adultery. So Harley figured he didn't know which sin was worse. He knew he shouldn't do it. Every ache of his guilty heart said so, but his loins sang a different song entirely.

Morena threw down the magazine. "See. He don't give a *fuck* about my feelings."

"I just don't know what to say to you. I'm sorry I fucked Cheryl." Harley snapped his thumbnail against his jeans. "But what else can I do but not do it?"

Mercedes brightened perceptibly. "Let's explore that, Harley. Just keep talking."

"I thought her name was Anne," Morena said.

"When I was a kid in high school, I thought that cars and pussy were it. I spent all my time after them and didn't get any. Then Pop left and I was sixteen. I worked all the time, Ma fucked the grocer for food and loans, and then I got married." Harley sat up and stared at Mercedes's hospital badge, the green and yellow of it like a feed-store hat against her black shirt. "We been over this trying to pin my doings on something that happened to me when I was a kid."

"There is no pinning, Harley. We're exploring different possibilities." Mercedes scribbled something in her yellow pad. Harley tried not to notice. Morena's chins started to tremble.

"I love Morena. Always have." Harley tried a quick look at Morena. She looked at the ceiling, still rocking in her chair and shaking her head.

"Harley, goddamnit. Who the fuck is Cheryl?" Harley

ducked, but the magazine drew blood from the corner of his eye. Morena hadn't even gotten up from the chair.

"Jesus Christ," Harley said. Mercedes handed him a tissue without blinking.

"Maybe we've taken this as far as we can for the day." Mercedes dropped her glasses onto her nose and wrote something on her pad again. "One of the next steps we take in couples therapy is reacquainting ourselves with each other. We have a choice of course, in what we would like to plan for your date night, but we've found that dance lessons work best for loosening couples from their normal routine. I assume you don't dance now."

Harley shook his head. Morena said "Fine. We dance then."

Harley drove home in silence. Morena carped at him, hit him once or twice when she thought he wasn't paying attention. Walking down the dirt path to the house, he noticed the bug-zapper shorting out—three short buzzes and a pause. It sounded to him like an SOS, from when he'd been a radio operator in the Corps. It seemed appropriate.

He sat next to her during the nighttime game shows and read from the Song of Songs, trying to get a feel for how Solomon dealt with these things. If he couldn't figure out what to do, and the twin does of her breasts and all that running stream-water under the Falls of En-gedi made Solomon lose his mind for a woman as well, what could he do? He knew it was what Mercedes would call rationalization. She would tell him that nothing or no one could *make* him do anything. He would have to do it himself. As with everything. It would have to be done himself.

When Morena fell asleep in front of the off-air signal, Harley walked outside to fix the bug-zapper. He knew it could wait, but he wouldn't be able to sleep anyway. Something useful could come from this night. Dancing, he thought. He had a vision of how painful that would be. Somebody he knew would be there as he tried to train his clumsy feet to steps normal men might have no trouble with. And yet again his troubles would be there for everyone to see. Harley sat heavily in the chair—fuck the zapper—and watched as cars passed by every hour or so. He listened to the night, to the infernal machine, until the three-zap pulse became a melody in his mind, and there he waltzed with his wife until he woke in the morning, covered in welts.

THE WAY IT IS
SCRIPTED, THE
WAY IT GOES

When Jasper touches the tip of my nose with her tongue after we kiss, I know she's serious. Sarita's block party, Jasper says, a great time to get to know the neighbors over cocktails, these people we barely acknowledge on the street. A hinky affair, I think, but Jasper calls in a babysitter and we're off.

It's been two hours since we dropped by Sarita's apartment, the rooms dim with candles and heady with sex, dark bodies moving in the corners. The whole time I've wanted to leave, and Jasper's wanted to play.

"You worry too much, Ken." Jasper's thickish jaw works over a wad of gum as she talks, a powerful chewing, the muscle striation that I imagine I can follow all the way down her chest and into her heart. It's been a year of trying, though, and I'm willing to spend more time, even to the point of this block party, even to this point of standing in Sarita's bathroom with the hot water on, talking about Jasper fucking another guy.

"This is a big step." It's not as if we haven't discussed it before, but the sight of Sarita's bouncing breasts and brown nipples, her frizz of hair hung over into my golf buddy Paul's face is raw and immutable fact, one I didn't prepare for. It's hard for me to imagine myself here, let alone Jasper, queen of privacy, who's already stripped to her panties in her drug-rush, beads of sweat running down her face and between her breasts.

"This'll help." Jasper reaches into her purse and hands me a largish white pill. Outside the door Sarita shrieks in ever-rising pitches. I swallow the pill with some fear, and she kisses my face all over, flicks the tip of my nose with her tongue in what is meant to be a ritual of calming. Except she's—we've—never done this before. Billows of steam rise from the sink and surround us in warmth. It's how I imagine a womb might feel, the sound of the water a tiny spit of rain in a great ocean of potential. We are there in the steam for a long time before we are joined by Sarita and Paul, looking for a shower, looking for us.

The way it is scripted, Jasper grasps Paul by the hand and pulls him toward her. Sarita does the same with me. The faucet is off but the seals need replacing, and each driplet echoes over the slick rasp of skin on skin. At one point we are on our knees, Sarita and I, like statuary at the feet of the Virgin, rubbing Jasper's thighs and behind with our wondrous, wonder-bound hands as Paul, my golfing buddy, ministers to Jasper, his hand at the dark thatch between her legs, both of them, all of us, awash in pleasure.

The way it goes, Sarita abandons pretense and buries her head in Jasper's crotch, pushing Paul aside and I am left dripping and limp yet with a rush of heat in my groin. I watch the pulse of muscle at Jasper's throat, the throb of Paul's penis waving about in front of me, and wondering what, exactly, that it is about the sound of water on porcelain that is so lonely, as Jasper cries out, again and again.

SPECIAL THANKS

Due to: Steve Almond, Tom Cobb, Ken and Nadine Darling, Ed Falco, Tim Gager, DeWitt Henry, Brian and Katie Laferte, Sue Miller, Cami Park, Mary Powers, Rod Siino. Thanks as well to the members of my writing communities Scrawl and Zoetrope for supporting my work over the last several years.

ABOUT THE AUTHOR

Rusty Barnes grew up in Mosherville, Pennsylvania. He received his BA from Mansfield University of Pennsylvania and his MFA from Emerson College. His flash fiction has appeared in many journals, among them *Pindeldyboz*, *Salt Flats Annual*, and *SmokeLong Quarterly*, and he edits the literary journal *Night Train*. He lives in Revere, Massachusetts with his family.